More from Hound and Bear

BY DICK GACKENBACH

Houghton Mifflin/Clarion Books/New York

FOR TED

LIBRARY OF CONGRESS CATALOGING IN PUBLICATION DATA

Gackenbach, Dick.   More from Hound and Bear.

SUMMARY: In two episodes, Hound is bailed out of his foolish decisions by Bear. In the final episode, Hound proves himself wiser than his lumbering friend.
[1. Friendship—Fiction.   2. Dogs—Fiction.
3. Bears—Fiction]   I. Title.
PZ7.G117Mm   [E]   79-4310   ISBN 0-395-28973-4

LOOK ALIKE

One day Bear went to see Hound.

Sensible Bear was surprised when he saw his friend.

On Hound's head was a wild and woolly mane.

"Why are you wearing that foolish mane?"

Bear asked.

"I want to look like Lion," answered Hound.

"But why?" Bear asked.

"Everyone says Lion is brave," said Hound.

"So, if I look like Lion, they will say I am brave too."

"Nonsense," said Bear.

In a few days, Bear went to visit Hound again.
Besides the mane, Hound was now wearing
dark glasses.
"Why are you wearing dark glasses?"
Bear wanted to know.
"I want to look like Raccoon," said Hound.
"Why?" asked Bear.
"Because everyone says Raccoon is wise,"
replied Hound.
"So if you look like Raccoon," said Bear,
"everyone will say you are wise too?"
"That's right," said Hound.
"What a noodle-head," muttered Bear.

On Bear's next visit, Hound still wore the mane.
He still wore the dark glasses too.
And now, to Bear's surprise, Hound was
tottering around on wooden stilts.
"Who are you supposed to look like today?"
Bear asked.
"Giraffe," Hound told him.
"Why?" questioned Bear. "No one ever said
Giraffe had wisdom or courage."
"No," agreed Hound, "But they do say he's tall."
"He is!" said Bear.
"Well then," said Hound, "since I already look wise
and brave, don't you think I should
look tall as well?"
"No," answered Bear. "Being tall has nothing
to do with being wise or brave."
Bear shook his head sadly and went home.

After Bear had gone, Hound went walking.
"Everyone must see how wonderful
I've become," he said.
But Hound could barely wobble
on his wooden stilts.
WOBBLE, WOBBLE, Hound went.
Then, CLUMPITTY, BUMPITTY,
Hound fell down a deep hole.
PLOP! He hit bottom like a stone.
"Somebody help," Hound shouted from below.
"Someone please get me out of here!"

Lion was the first to hear Hound's
call for help.
But Lion just clung to a tree
and did nothing.
"Why can't you help me?" Hound shouted.
"I'm afraid," Lion yelled back. "I might
fall in too."
"But," said Hound, "everyone says
you're fearless."
"I never said that!" said Lion.
"Oh, you ninny," shouted Hound.
"I'm sorry," said Lion.
Then he hurried away.

"Help! Somebody! Anybody! Help!"
Hound continued to call.
Soon Raccoon heard his cries.
"You are clever," said Hound.
"Get me out of this hole."
"I know nothing about getting
a hound out of a hole,"
Raccoon told Hound. "But I can take a lid
off a garbage can if that will help."
"You cabbage-head!" shouted Hound.

CABBAGE-HEAD!

"If that's how you feel," said Raccoon,
"then phooey to you!"
And Raccoon went away.
Hound still bellowed, "Help."
"Save me," he shouted
as loud as he could.

In time Giraffe heard Hound call.

But Giraffe was no help either.

"Oh dear," Giraffe told Hound.

"I have a fear of high places."

"But," said Hound, "I am down a hole, not up a tree."

"I know that," said Giraffe. "But if I looked down that hole,
 I would get dizzy and faint. I would fall
 on top of you."

"You nincompoop!" said Hound.

"Sorry," said Giraffe.

Meanwhile Bear began to wonder
what had happened to his friend.
So Bear came looking for Hound.
When he heard Hound calling from the hole,
Bear went to the edge and shouted,
"Is that my tall, wise and brave friend
down there?"
Hound was very happy to hear Bear's voice.
"Oh good Bear," he cried. "Please get me
out of here."

Bear ran home for a rope. He returned
to the hole and tossed the rope down to Hound.
"WHEW," sighed Hound after Bear pulled him up.
"Am I glad to see you."
"I came looking for you," said Bear, "because I have
something for you."

Hound was delighted. Not only was he out
of the hole, he was getting a present as well.
"What did you bring me?" he wanted to know.
"These," said Bear as he placed two long ears on
Hound's head.
"What are the ears for?" Hound asked.
"Because everyone says you have been
acting like a silly jackass," said Bear.
"And if you act like one, I think you should
look like one."
"Oh dear," said Hound.

THE FAVOR

Hound came to visit Bear every Tuesday.

All afternoon the two friends would sit
in the rockers on Bear's shady porch.
One Tuesday, while they rocked back and forth,
Hen came by.

"Will you do me a favor?" she asked.

"Not me," said Hound. "I don't do favors."

"That's silly," Bear told Hound.

"Favors are nice things to do."

"Pooh, says you," said Hound.

"What can I do for you?" Bear asked Hen.

"I need a wagon to carry my eggs to market,"
 Hen told Bear.

"Take mine," said Bear.

"Thank you, Bear," said Hen.
 Then Hen put all her eggs in Bear's red wagon
 and continued on her way to market.

"Wait and see," warned Hound.

"You'll be sorry you gave that chicken
 your red wagon."

"Oh, fiddle-faddle,"
 said Bear.

Soon Hen met Alligator.

"Do me a favor, Hen?" said Alligator.

"Glad to," replied Hen.

"There's an itch in the middle of my back,"
he told her. "Please scratch it for me."
Hen fluttered up on Alligator's
long back and began
to scratch.

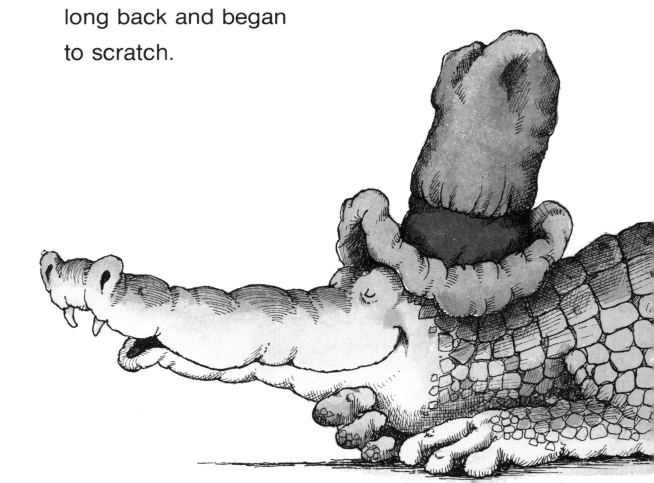

Her sharp chicken toes did
a fine job.
"Ah-h-h-h," Alligator sighed.
"That felt good."

Alligator was so pleased with Hen's favor
that he didn't mind at all when
Porcupine asked one of him.
"What can I do for you?" asked Alligator.
"Give me a lift across the pond," said Porcupine.
"Sure thing," said Alligator. "Hop on!"
Porcupine held tight to Alligator,
and Alligator carried him swiftly
across the water.
"Many thanks," said Porcupine.
"My pleasure," said Alligator.

On the other side of the pond,
Porcupine met Farmer Mule.
"You are just the fellow I've been looking for,"
said Mule. "Will you do me a favor?"
"What is it?" asked Porcupine.
"With all your quills and spines,
bees can't sting you," Mule said.
"Will you gather the honey from the hives for me?"

"Sure," said Porcupine.
And so
Porcupine removed
the golden honey
from Mule's beehives.
When he had finished,
Mule gave him
half a dozen jars
of honey
for himself.
"Thank you," said Porcupine.
"But," he wondered,
"how can I carry
the six jars home?"

At that moment Hen came by.

She was on her way home from market,

and Bear's red wagon was empty.

Hen stopped.

"Do you need help?" she asked.

"I do," said Porcupine.

"Put your jars in the wagon," Hen told him.

"We'll pull together."

So Hen and Porcupine pulled and pushed

the load of honey all the way

to Porcupine's door.

Porcupine was so grateful that he gave Hen

a jar of the golden honey.

"For your kindness," he said.

"That's very nice of you," said Hen.

"I have a dear friend who's wild about honey."

Hen took the jar and waved goodbye.

Then she went straight to Bear's house.

"Here's your wagon back," Hen told Bear,

"and with a big jar of honey in it."

Bear was delighted.

"Humpf," said Hound when he saw the honey.

"Bear has all the luck."

"Something nice could happen to you, too,"

said Hen, "if you did a favor now and then."

"Do you really think so?" said Hound.

"Take my word for it," said Hen.

Later, when Bear asked Hound,
"Do me a big favor?"
Hound answered right away.
"Sure!" he said. "My pleasure!"
"Good," said Bear.
"Come help me eat this honey."
"Whoopee!" said Hound.

AN ORDINARY EVERYDAY NUT

Hound rushed home from the Fair.

"Look," he called to Bear. "See what I bought at the Fair."

"It's an ordinary nut," said Bear. "A plain walnut."

"Oh no it isn't," said Hound. "It's a wishing nut."

Bear laughed at Hound.

"*You* are a nut if you believe that," he said.

Bear's teasing made Hound cross.

"You big booby!" Hound snapped at Bear.

This made Bear cross.

"Double booby!" Bear called Hound.

Hound stuck his nose high in the air.

He walked out of Bear's house and slammed the door.

No sooner had Hound gone than Bear was sorry.

"I was wrong to laugh at my friend," he said.

So Bear sat down and wrote Hound a letter.

The letter arrived in the next morning's mail.

Hound tore open the envelope and read the letter.

It said: *Let's make up. Yours truly, Bear*

Hound was ready to make up too.

He ran to Bear's house as fast as he could.

"I'm so glad you came," said Bear.

"Please stay for lunch."

"Don't mind if I do," said Hound.

"I'll make your favorite dish, macaroni pie," said Bear.

"Great," said Hound.

"I don't like being mad at you," said Bear.

"Nor I with you," said Hound. "In fact, I was wishing
for a letter from you when one came."

"No fooling," gasped Bear.

"And I was wishing you would ask me
to stay for lunch," said Hound.

"You don't say," said Bear.

"And I wished for macaroni pie too," said Hound.

"Imagine that," said Bear.

"So you see, all my wishes came true," said Hound.

"So what?" said Bear.

"So it proves my nut is a real wishing nut," said Hound.

Bear threw his hands in the air.

"That doesn't prove a thing," he shouted.

"Let's settle this once and for all."

"How?" Hound wanted to know.

"Make a wish," said Bear. "Make the most important wish you can think of, and then we will see if it comes true."

Hound took a minute or two to think about his most important wish.

"I'm ready," he said at last.

"All right, then," said Bear. "Make your wish."

"I wish," said Hound,

"that Bear will be my friend forever."

Bear blushed.

"That wish will come true," he promised Hound.

"You can count on it."

"In that case," said Hound,

"I won't need this nut any more."

There was a loud crack.

Hound had broken the nut in two.

"Half for you," he said to Bear.

"And half for me."